THE ADVENTURES OF THE TOOTH BRIGADE ™

WORDS: SHARON AZULA
PICTURES: ANDY AZULA

It Helps To Play™

Late one afternoon, a huge storm blew in.
Farmer Flanderberry's tumbleweeds were tossed high into the sky.

Anything that could fly
was told not to.

It was so windy, even the Tooth Fairy was worried.
Especially since she was scheduled to go to the top
of Tippy Top Mountain that night.

The Tooth Fairy knew lots of kids were depending
on her, so she decided to fly anyway.

She had almost made it to the Sticky Swamp when a tumbleweed fell out of the sky and dropped right on top of her.

She was stuck and it would be a **looooooooooooooooooong** time before she could get out.

Just then, she heard voices in the distance
and saw three shadows approaching.

Monster shadows.

But these weren't just any monsters. These monsters were three friends practicing for a talent show.

There was Potato, who loved to juggle food.

There was Blue, who could ride a unicycle.

And there was Ollie, who loved to sing.

Let's hear you sing, Ollie!

IT'S THE TUMBLEWEED FAIRY!
NO. I'M THE TOOTH FAIRY, STUCK IN THIS TUMBLEWEED.

So. The Tooth Brigade set out on their adventure.

First they squished and squashed through the Sticky Swamp.

Next, they had to find a way to cross
Crocodile Creek, which was full of cranky crocodiles.

Great job, Ollie! Your singing made
the crocodiles dive underwater.

After that, Ollie, Potato and Blue had no problem hopping across.

At long last, they made it to the tippy top of Tippy Top mountain.

Potato, Ollie and Blue
sneakily snuck down the hallway.

They tiptoed into the bedroom, careful not to wake anyone, especially Sir Barks-a-Lot, who was snoring at the foot of the bed.

They searched and searched, late into the night.

They looked inside the fish tank.

They looked in the rock collection.

They looked through the books.

They looked behind the TV.

They looked everywhere they could think of, even under the pillow.

Ollie, you did look under the pillow, right?

Sir Barks-a-Lot started barking up a storm!

BARK
BARK
BARK

HEY, DOGGIE! LOOK AT ME!

CHOMP CHOMP CHOMP

Sir Barks-a-Lot dove under the bed.

The Tooth Brigade breathed a huge sigh of relief.
Wheeeeew! Thank goodness the Tooth Fairy didn't see all that!

And so, on that night, Blue, Potato and Ollie became the very first official members of The Tooth Brigade, the Tooth Fairy's most valuable helpers.

The End.
(Until the next adventure.)

Tooth Fairy's Guide

When you lose your teeth,
you may have lots of questions.
I've got the answers.

WHEN DO BABY TEETH FALL OUT?

When they are good and ready!
That usually happens when you are around
5 or 6 years old. And by the time you are all
grown up, you will have lost around 20 teeth!
Each will be replaced with a permanent adult tooth!

DOES IT HURT WHEN A TOOTH COMES OUT?

Usually not much or not
at all! It will get really
wiggly. When it does,
you can start wiggling
it to help loosen it even more.

IS IT GOING TO BLEED A LOT?

Sometimes it doesn't bleed at all. Sometimes it might
bleed a little. But it should stop bleeding pretty quickly.

DO YOU EVER FORGET TO COME? OR MISS A HOUSE?

Forget? No, never. But sometimes, very, very rarely, I can't make it. Sometimes the weather is bad or it's just a super busy night! That's why I need **The Tooth Brigade!** They can keep your tooth safe until I get there.

WHAT HAPPENS IF A TOOTH FALLS OUT AND GETS **LOST**?! OR GETS **SWALLOWED**?!

Guess what? That happens a lot. Just write me a note or download a tooth ticket from **www.thetoothbrigade.com** Then give either one to The Tooth Brigade. It counts as a lost tooth, but only when you can't find your tooth or you've swallowed it!

GOOD FOR ONE
Missing tooth
☐ Lost it
☐ Get Swallowed
☐ fell in sink
☐ other
The Tooth Fairy will count this as a lost tooth
TICKET

DO DOGS HEAR BETTER THAN PEOPLE?

They do! By a lot. Maybe that's why when Ollie sings, dogs always run away. It's a good bet Ollie can sing super high notes!

WHAT EXACTLY IS A TUMBLEWEED?

A tumbleweed is a plant or weed. It's all dried up and looks like a dead bush or a bunch of twigs. When the wind blows, the dried up plant tumbles away, so it is called a tumbleweed!

Lost Tooth Tracker

Use this chart to keep track of all the teeth you lose. Write down the date each time you lose a baby tooth.

The Tooth Brigade can take care of your lost teeth too!

If you would like to have Ollie, Potato or Blue keep your lost teeth safe, go to **www.thetoothbrigade.com** to order your own member of The Tooth Brigade.

A portion of all proceeds will be donated to charities who provide dental care for children in need.

To Sophie and Jackson
for their endless curiosity.

Tippy Top Mountain

sticky Swamp

random Mountains

Crocodile Creek

Tumbleweed Farm

The Tooth Brigade™
Story and illustrations © 2019 It Helps To Play

First Printing 2019

ISBN 978-1-7340471-0-3

Published by It Helps To Play™

Visit us at www.thetoothbrigade.com

That Way

Tippy Top Mountain

Tooth Fairy's House

This Way